MW01109595

EX LIBRIS

BP25 © 1992 Quality Artworks

This book belongs to

Samantha Dorothy

With love,

Mother

March 30, 1994

Rumpelstiltskin

BY

The Brothers Grimm

Retold by Jennifer Greenway

ILLUSTRATED BY

Gary Cooley

ARIEL BOOKS

ANDREWS AND McMEEL

KANSAS CITY

Library of Congress Cataloging-in-Publication Data

Rumpelstilzchen (Grimm version). English.
    Rumpelstiltskin / the Brothers Grimm ; illustrated by Gary Cooley.
        p.   cm.
    "Ariel books."
    Summary: A strange little man helps the miller's daughter spin
straw into gold for the king on the condition that she will give him
her first-born child.
    ISBN 0-8362-4922-4 : $6.95
    [1. Fairy tales. 2. Folklore—Germany.] I. Grimm, Jacob.
1785–1863. II. Grimm, Wilhelm, 1786–1859. III. Cooley, Gary, ill.
IV. Title.
PZ8.R89Cm   1992
398.2—dc20
[E]   91–34397
                                                                    CIP
                                                                     AC

Design: Susan Hood and Mike Hortens
Art Direction: Armand Eisen, Mike Hortens, and Julie Phillips
Art Production: Lynn Wine
Production: Julie Miller and Lisa Shadid

Rumpelstiltskin

Once long ago there lived a miller who had a beautiful daughter. One day the king of the land happened to be passing by the mill. To make himself seem important to the king, the miller boasted that his daughter knew how to spin straw into gold.

The king, who liked gold very much, was most impressed.

7

"I should like to meet this daughter of yours," the king said to the miller. "Bring her to my palace tomorrow morning, and we shall see if what you say is true."

When the miller told his daughter what he had done, she was very upset. But there was nothing she could do. So early the next morning she presented herself at the king's palace.

8

The king led her into a large room that was completely filled with straw. Then he showed her to a spinning wheel and said, "Now you must get to work. But first, let me tell you this. If you have not spun all the straw into gold by tomorrow morning, you will pay with your life." Then the king left the room and locked the door behind him.

As soon as the king was gone, the miller's

beautiful daughter began to cry, despairing that she had no idea how to spin straw into gold. Just as she was sure there was no hope for her, the door of the room creaked open.

A strange little man came walking in. He looked at her and said, "Tell me, miller's daughter, why are you crying?"

"The king has ordered me to spin this straw into gold," she sobbed. "Unless I do he will have me put to death. And I have no idea how to do it!"

"Oh, that is no problem," replied the strange little man. "What will you give me if I do it for you?" The miller's daughter stared at him in astonishment. "I . . . I will give you my necklace!" she replied.

10

"Very well," said the little man and he accepted the necklace. Then he sat down at the spinning wheel and quickly set it whirring. Round and round it turned. Soon the bobbin was full of gold thread. Then the little man put another bobbin on the spinning wheel. Soon that one was full, too.

And on he went all night long until he had spun all the straw into shining gold thread!

The miller's daughter was overjoyed, and she thanked the little man with all her heart. Then, as the sun rose over the horizon, the strange little man vanished.

Soon the king came to see if the miller's daughter had spun the straw into gold. When he saw all the gold thread, he was amazed and delighted. Yet the sight of so much gold only made the king greedier. So he led the miller's daughter to another room.

This room was larger than the first and also filled with straw. "You must spin all this straw into gold by morning," the king told the miller's daughter, "or you will lose your life."

As soon as the king had gone and locked the door behind him, the miller's daughter burst into tears.

Then the door slowly opened, and in walked the same strange little man.

"Good day, miller's daughter," he said. "What will you give me if I spin the straw into gold for you this time?"

"I . . . I will give you my ring!" she replied.

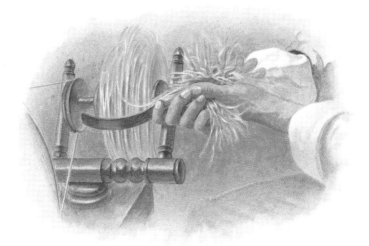

So the strange little man accepted the ring from the young woman's finger. Then he sat down at the spinning wheel and began spinning the straw into gold. And as soon as he was finished he disappeared.

Soon after dawn, the king came to see if the miller's daughter had completed her task. His eyes grew wide at the brilliance of the gold. But it only made him want to have more. So he led the miller's daughter to a third room.

This room was even larger, and it was piled to the ceiling with straw.

"You must spin all this straw into gold before the sun rises tomorrow," the king told the miller's daughter. "If you fail, you will lose your life. But if you succeed I will marry you and make you my wife." The king was thinking to himself that though she was only a miller's daughter, he would never find a richer wife anywhere.

After the king had left the miller's daughter and locked the door behind him, the strange little man once again appeared.

"What will you give me this time for spinning all this straw into gold?" he asked the miller's daughter.

The girl began to sob. "I have nothing left to give you," she answered.

"It is all right," said the little man. "Just promise me this: that when you are queen, you will give me your first child."

The miller's daughter hesitated. Then she gave the strange little man her promise. "Who knows if I shall ever be queen," she thought. "Besides, if I do not agree, then I will surely lose my life tomorrow."

So the little man sat down at the spinning wheel and set it turning. On and on it whirred until all the straw in the room had been spun into shining gold. The next morning the king came in and saw the immense gold treasure shimmering like the light of a thousand suns. He married the miller's beautiful daughter that very day. She was now a queen with fine robes and a crown on her head.

Within a year, the queen gave birth to a beautiful baby boy. She was overjoyed to have a child of her own. In her happiness, she forgot her promise to the strange little man.

One day, as the queen was playing with her baby son, the little man visited her.

"I have come to claim what you promised me," he said, stretching out his arms toward the child.

The queen was horrified. "Please do not take my little son," she pleaded. "I will give you anything—anything you wish. Only leave me my son!"

Then she offered the strange little man all the wealth and riches in the kingdom, if he would only spare her child.

At first, the little man refused. But the queen began to weep so sorrowfully that he took pity on her. "Very well," he said. "I will give you three days to guess my name. If you do so in that time, you may keep your little son. But if you fail, the child must be mine." And with that the strange little man vanished.

The queen stayed awake all night. She thought of every name she had ever heard. Then she took her candle and went to the palace library and searched through all the books for strange and unusual names.

The next morning when the little man appeared, the queen began asking him, "Is your name Peter? Is your name John? Is your name Charlemagne?"

Each time the little man replied, "Oh, no! That is not my name!"
Then the queen recited all the names she knew one after the other. But to each one the little man replied, "Oh, no! That is not my name!" Finally, she could think of no more names and the little man went away.

The queen summoned to her all the learned men of the kingdom and asked them to tell her all the strange and unusual names they had ever heard. She sent out her servants far and wide to collect as many odd names as they could.

When the little man came the next day, she asked him, "Is your name Big-Boots? Is your name Turtle-Beak? Can your name be Mutton-Chop or Crooked-Knees?"

But to each name the little man replied as before, "Oh, no! That is not my name!"

The queen did not know what to do.

On the third day, one of the queen's servants came to her and told a curious story.

"I searched far and wide, but I could not

find a single new name," the man began.
"Then on my way back through the
mountains I came upon a tiny cottage. A
fire was blazing in front of it, and a little
man was dancing around the fire on one
foot. As he danced, he sang this song:

I'll rest tomorrow and bake today
Then I'll take the queen's son away.
For no one will ever guess who I am
And that Rumpelstiltskin is my name!"

The queen clapped her hands for joy.

When the little man came the next morning, she asked him, "Is your name Henry?"

"No!" he replied.

"Is your name Roland?"

"No!"

"Then can your name be . . . Rumpelstiltskin?"

The little man's mouth fell open. "Who told you that? Who told you that?" he shrieked.

And he became so cross, he tugged at his little beard and stamped his foot. He stamped so hard that the ground cracked open beneath him and swallowed him up! And that was the last anyone ever saw of Rumpelstiltskin!